The Friend Ship

MARLOW

HENLEY

DORNEY

WINDSOR

RUNNYMEAD

The Friend Ship

Rachel Macdonald
&
Shiplake CofE Primary School

CITY OF LONDON

KEW

WESTMINSTER

GREENWICH

HAMPTON COURT

The Little Ship has always dreamt of one day being a Big Ship. But there is still so far to go on their journey to become one! They have already sailed across the cold, harsh Atlantic Ocean, over rough waves into the North Sea and into the Thames Estuary. But with six lessons to learn before they can be a Big Ship, how will they find the energy to keep going? They remember the advice they were given at the start of their adventure...

"To be a Big Ship you need to know the six greatest values that will help you grow."

Filled with purpose, the Little Ship puffs upstream and takes in all the sights of the City of London as they chug along.

Look, the Tower of London… and the London Eye!

Then they see a building with a fantastic clock and glide over to take a look. It's the Houses of Parliament!

The Little Ship heads to the bank to moor up but a big brown river rat jumps onto their deck, holding out their claws for a mooring fee. The Little Ship doesn't have any money so agrees to take the rat to the South Bank of the river instead of making the payment.

When the Little Ship returns back into the shadows of the Houses of Parliament they moor up next to some other boats. Whilst talking to an old canal house boat, it reveals that the brown rat has tricked the Little Ship. There is no fee to pay!

The Little Ship feels so foolish and hurt but then realises that this is perhaps one of the lessons they have to learn…

***Truthfulness* must be the first value that I need to learn on my journey.**

The next day the Little Ship wakes with the sun to continue their adventure up the Thames. They power past Kew and the beautiful gardens and then Hampton Court where Henry VIII once lived with some of his many wives.

As the Little Ship puffs round a bend, they see a sign for Runnymede and notice a circle of ornate, metal chairs in a clearing to the side of the river. The Little Ship is intrigued and when an electric blue kingfisher flashes past they call out to ask about the unexpected sight.

The kingfisher explains that Runnymede is where the Magna Carta was signed in 1215. This document has been the foundation of laws and human rights around the world.

The kingfisher continues to tell the Little Ship about *'The Golden Rule'*; to treat others as you would wish to be treated yourself. But they are interrupted by a shiny new boat zooming up the river, barging little boats out of the way into the brambles. The Little Ship and the kingfisher are left soaked and battered in its wake.

The Little Ship feels so angry that the little boats have been treated like they are not as important as the more powerful boat. The Little Ship promises to never behave like that no matter how big they get. They make a promise to always treat others with respect and equality.

***Equality* must be the second value I need to learn if I am going to make my way in the world.**

The Little Ship reaches Windsor and what sights they can see! On one side of the bank is Eton College - one of the oldest schools in England. And there through the trees on the other side is Windsor Castle!

When they were small, the Little Ship had dreamt of meeting Queen Elizabeth II, the longest serving Queen of England. Now they thought all of her wisdom could help them learn their next lesson.

They edge closer to the bank but one of the Queen's swans flys towards them and warns the Little Ship that a storm is coming and the river can flood quickly. It is particularly dangerous for watercraft like the Little Ship who are trying to head upstream. They need to keep going and get to a safe spot.

The Little Ship feels torn about what they want to do and what they need to do. It's so hard making decisions all by themselves. But they know that the sensible choice is to keep going to learn another lesson.

Wisdom is the third value that I must learn if I am to keep safe and sound in my travels.

"The swan warned me if I stay
I may never get away!
The river will start flowing quickly,
So I must talk to myself strictly.
I know that I need to be WISE,
If I am ever to increase in size."

The Little Ship steams past the Olympic rowers on Dorney Lake and navigates through the narrow lock at Maidenhead. After the lock, they pass the formal gardens of the Cliveden estate and the wildflowers of Cock Marsh in Cookham.

As they arrive in Marlow, the storm finally breaks. Lightning suddenly strikes and they're sure they can see Mary Shelley's monster in the shadows of Higginson Park. The Little Ship is so scared and feels very lost, but they focus on using all of their might and courage to battle the stormy Thames and continue upstream.

The Little Ship arrives at Temple Lock but this time they are confused. There are two locks! The Little Ship doesn't know what to do and the rain is heavier and the thunder is louder than ever before. The Little Ship starts to panic.

Just then the lock keeper comes to help the Little Ship, shouting instructions through the pounding rain and choppy water. The Little Ship stops and listens hard, takes deep breaths and follows the lock keeper's advice.

Finally, they steer through and make their way to a quiet siding of the river to rest, regulate and get some peace so they can keep going on their journey.

Peace is the fourth value that I must learn if I want to hear the important things in life.

The Little Ship has travelled so far. They have learnt about history, geography, and most importantly they have learnt four of their lessons; truthfulness, equality, wisdom, and peace.

But the Little Ship can't ever remember feeling so tired. The Little Ship slows and comes to a stop at Henley Bridge, pausing for a moment to watch the rowers practising for the regatta and the pleasure cruisers chugging up and down.

But they begin to worry, their wood is splintering and water is slowly seeping in. Maybe this means they will never become a Big Ship after all?

"I am still so tired and I've lost my glee,
Atlantic Ocean to the North Sea,
Palaces, bridges, oxbows and all of the locks
I think I just need to stop
Only four lessons have I learnt so far
I don't know what the next two are."

Trying to stay calm, the Little Ship closes their eyes and tries not to think about sinking to the bottom of the Thames. Just then a teacher and her class wander across the walkway and see the Little Ship. The children see how tired and beaten the Little Ship looks and they want to do something to help save them from sinking.

The children plead with their parents and teachers and they soon find a way to take the Little Ship home with them to their school. With some care and attention the Little Ship becomes an important member of school life.

Compassion is the fifth value that I must learn so that I can help others as they have helped me.

The Little Ship knew they had not learned all of their lessons. They felt really disappointed thinking they would never be a Big Ship after all. Although the Little Ship was sad sometimes, they still brought joy to the young children by letting them play on their creaky floorboards and dance around their mast.

All of the children enjoy hearing the Little Ship's tales about the Thames, the North sea, and the Atlantic ocean. Stories about the beautiful buildings and sights they saw along the way and how scared and excited they felt during the journey enchant the children, filling their imaginations with dreams of adventure and learning.

"To be a Big Ship you need to know
The six greatest values that will help you grow.
These were the words that had started this goal
But now I have to adapt to another role.
It's not what I thought i'd be
But I know I bring joy and I'm happy."

Little Ship

Then, one day a child sat silently on the ship - sad because they had no friends to play with. The Little Ship felt the little child's pain; understood the feelings of loneliness and despair.

The Little Ship told the child about their amazing adventures and of the five lessons they had learned, but also about the missing lesson.

Excitedly, the child turned to the ship and said:*"I think I know what the last lesson is. You let us all play on you and we come to you when we are sad. You are everyone's best friend."*

The Little Ship looked into the child's kind face and then it struck them - they had learned their final lesson! Along with truthfulness, equality, wisdom, peace, and compassion, the Little Ship knew that one of the most important things in life was... friendship!

And from that day forward they were no longer the Little Ship.

Or the Big Ship.

They were the FRIEND *Ship*.

Teachers Notes — Curriculum Conversation Starters

Geography

The Little Ship travels up the River Thames on their journey.
The Thames is the longest river in England.

- Can you look on a map and find it?
- Where is the source of the River Thames?
- Where is the mouth of the River Thames? What is it called in the book? Which sea does it flow into?
- The Little Ship talks about traveling across the Atlantic. Where on your map is the Atlantic Ocean? Where do you think the Little Ship came from and which way did they get into the North Sea?
- Can you draw a map and write a little story about where they came from, what languages they might speak and who they left behind?

The Little Ship came into England from the North Sea. If we look on a map, England is part of the United Kingdom (UK).

- What are the four **countries** that make up the UK? What are the capital cities of those countries?
- If we look at London in more detail, can you find the counties that sit around London; what are they called? What are the main features of those counties? (Roads, parks, airports)
- How many counties does the Little Ship travel through?
- Could you create a sight-seeing guide for the exact journey that the Little Ship made from the Thames Estuary. Which sights would you include and what would you say about them?

History

As the Little Ship travels up the Thames, they mention some special places and significant people from the past. Can you find them in the book and write them down?

Do you know who they are and why they might be important to our history? Are there some names and places that you didn't know about until now?

Let's dig a little deeper...

Choose one of the following places or people:

- The Houses of Parliament
- Henry VIII
- Runnymede
- Queen Elizabeth II

We'd like you to do some research and then tell your friends / class / parent / teacher all about what you have learned.

Consider including:

- Why is this person / place important to history?
- What are the key dates associated with the place / person?
- Are there some other people that are also important in the story of this place / person?
- Is the story of the person / place still important to us now? Can you tell us why?

Printed in Great Britain
by Amazon